Poppy's Place

Adorably Sweet and Steamy DDLG Instalove Romance

Little Lovelies Playroom
Book 1

Kimmy Cain

Surrendered Press

Surrendered Press

Poppy's Place

Copyright © 2024 by Kimmy Cain

All rights reserved.

No part of this book may be reproduced in any form or by any electronic or mechanical means, including information storage and retrieval systems, without written permission from the author, except for the use of brief quotations in a book review.

Contents

1. Poppy — 1
2. Carter — 7
3. Poppy — 13
4. Carter — 19
5. Poppy — 27
6. Carter — 31
7. Poppy — 41
8. Carter — 49
9. Poppy — 55
10. Carter — 67
11. Poppy — 77
12. Carter — 83
13. Poppy — 93
14. Carter — 101
15. Poppy — 109
    Epilogue — 115

Chapter 1

Poppy

There was a crowd of people by the pick-up counter when Cassie walked in. She came straight to me, throwing her arms around me and hanging from me, practically collapsing over me. "Please tell me you ordered for me, Pop. I need caffeine, stat."

I hugged her back and smiled. "Yes, Cassie. Of course, I ordered for you. I wasn't about to waste our quick visit by making you stand in line again."

Just then, the barista screamed out my name and slid two coffees and two slices of banana bread across the counter.

"Ooh, that couple over there is leaving. I'll grab the

table if you grab the food." Just as quickly as she arrived, Cassie took off to save our seats.

When I dropped into the chair across from her with a tray of our snacks and drinks, I felt as exhausted as she looked. "So why the urgency around our meeting today? Or did you just want to see my pearly whites?"

Cassie bit off a corner of her pastry and grinned. "You know how much I love your smile, but I need a favor." She wrapped both hands around her warm mug and held it to her face. "And I'll owe you forever."

That didn't sound good. "What do you need this time, Cass?"

"Can you host the Little Lovelies tonight?" It was her turn to flash her pearly whites at me. "I know you had to do it last time, but my place is an absolute mess, and there's no way I can get it ready for playgroup tonight."

"Cassie…" I hated whining, but sometimes it couldn't be stopped. "I have to move all my furniture and unpack the bins. What if I go help you get your apartment ready before anyone else arrives?"

"That's really nice, but there's no way I can make it work. I've been experimenting with some new candles, and I have supplies set up all over the place. I can't just start moving everything around or it'll be ruined."

"Really?" I frowned, knowing that nothing would get ruined by moving it out of the way, but I understood her situation. Even though it was a pain, it was easiest for me to host because my living room and dining room combo were set up in a way that if I pushed everything to the walls, we had a pretty nice playspace.

"Pretty please with poppies on top?" She clasped her hands under her chin and begged with her eyes as convincingly as her mouth.

"Fine. I'll do it again, but I'm not hosting for the next... five playdates." I crossed my arms over my chest and felt my lower lip jut out, even though Cassie was completely immune to my sad face. The only time I could get away with anything was if I was at the club and one of the Dungeon Monitors, or Daycare Masters as we liked to call them, wanted me to put my toys away before I was ready or if I needed someone to read us a story. "But we really need to find a better way to host playdates. Maybe we can rent a permanent room at the club so we don't ever have to clean it up?"

"Thank you, thank you, thank you!" Cassie finally relaxed and took a drink of her latte. "I knew you'd help. And yeah, wouldn't that be awesome? A place where we could just show up anytime we wanted and have our toys out and ready to go."

I sighed and took a drink too. "Someday I'll buy a house with a basement that can be a special playroom just for the Little Lovelies."

"And when you do, I promise to go over once a week and help clean it so it's not all on you."

"Thanks, Cass." I broke off another piece of the banana bread and slid it into my mouth. Bean Box made the best banana bread. Even better than mine. "So, everyone will be there at six?"

She was chewing, so she held up her finger, asking me to wait. "Yeah. I'll bring dinner so you don't have to worry about that. Just get the play area ready, and leave the rest to me."

I raised an eyebrow, trying to look stern but failing miserably when I giggled. "I want chicken strips, mac and cheese, and cookies." I pursed my lips and thought about it. "Actually, not the cookies. I'll ask Kylie if she can bring a cake. She was baking all weekend, so I'm sure she has something."

"You're the best, Poppy." Cassie wadded up her crumb-filled napkin and stood up to leave. "I've got to get back to the store, but I'll be there at five forty-five with dinner. If you need anything else, call me."

I stood up and gave her a hug before she ran toward the door. Cassie was a whirlwind who never slowed down, and her apartment showed the aftermath of the tornado that was my best friend. "See you tonight. And drive carefully."

Once she was gone, I quickly finished my pastry and the rest of my coffee before heading back to my car. It was parked right across the street, but I'd been in such a hurry when I parked that I didn't pay attention to the For Sale sign on the building where I was parked.

But after the conversation I'd just had with Cassie, it was all I could see. Right there in the middle of Tiny Seeds Pre-K and Childcare Center was a big, red For Sale sign. I crossed the street and went to investigate.

The door was locked, and when I peeked in through the window, there was a mess of papers on the ground in front of the reception desk and a small chair was turned over. It seemed like the building had been abandoned.

Without hesitating, I dialed the number on the sign and held my breath. The money my parents gave me from my college fund had been burning a hole in my pocket since I graduated two years earlier. Partly because I didn't know what to do with it, but also because I wanted to do something special with it. And as I read the sales listing and saw that the 2000-square-foot building had a large playroom with parent viewing center, a bathroom, a kitchenette, and a reception area on the first floor and a two-bedroom apartment right above it, it felt as special as special could be.

In fact, I didn't bother leaving a message when I was sent to the agent's voicemail. I just snapped a photo of the listing and drove two miles down the road to the broker's office to talk to someone in person.

Since I was always the one in charge of providing a place space for my Little friends, buying the building was as much for my benefit as theirs. And not having to clean up our toys and stuffies after every playdate was just the cherry on the most special sundae of all.

Chapter 2

Carter

(Three Weeks Later)

I was in my office when Rory poked his head around the doorway. "I'm hungry."

Looking up from my computer screen, I shrugged. "Okay."

"Let's go get a muffin." He stepped farther into the room. "Your treat."

Rolling my eyes, I turned back to my computer. "You make millions in commission every year. You don't need to hit me up for free snacks. Just go over there and buy a damn muffin." I looked up again, remembering that I skipped lunch. "Actually, get me one too. I'm starving."

"See." He slipped his hands into his pockets and walked over to me. "Just go with me. I'll buy, but they give us the best service when you're with me."

"That better not be true." I stood up and stretched, loath to admit that a walk and some fresh air sounded pretty good. "My staff treats everyone like the owner... at least, they'd better."

Now he rolled his eyes. "Yeah, they do. Just come with me. I want to run something by you."

"Of course you do." I put my computer to sleep and then walked around the desk. "I'll go, but since they'll give it to us for free, you better put a fat tip in that jar before we leave."

Rory grinned. "I'm about to give you a fat tip, so let's go."

It was a warm day, with the sun shining high in the sky. I grew up in Sunnyvale, California and never planned to leave. It was just too perfect 98% of the year. And the other 2% was still better than what most regions considered a good day. We were about ten steps out of the building we shared office space in when he went for it. "Okay, I have an idea."

"Go ahead." Rory had a lot of ideas, and I seemed to be his favorite sounding board, so I just played along. Some of them were actually pretty good and had made me millions over the years. "Lay it on me."

"You know how the new stadium project was just approved for development and should be finished in a few years?" When I nodded, his eyes lit up. "Well, I'm thinking we should start buying some of the old houses and condos around here as short-term rentals. We can rehab them over the next year and make a killing once the stadium opens up. I've found a few places I really like, but to do this right, I want to bring in a few partners."

I raised an eyebrow and turned to him. "And I'm one of the chosen few you'll allow to give you money for this little endeavor?"

He clapped my shoulder and chuckled. "Exactly. What do you say, man? I've got several listings I think we should check out. They might not all still be available, but if we can get a few deals in the pipeline, then I'll manage the renovations so we can get them rentable within a few months. By the time the stadium opens, we could already be in the green."

I had many businesses, but most were retail or commercial office space. Nothing residential. And I was intrigued by the idea. "Yeah, I'd consider that. Find a few places you think could work and then let me know what the numbers look like."

"I knew you'd love the idea." Rory was almost giddy. "You always know a good proposal when you hear one."

A few minutes later, we walked into one of my coffee shops. I had three franchises in the area, but this one was walking distance from my office building in the charming downtown district. I'd always loved the area and planned to acquire other businesses anyway, so it just made sense. "Anything around here?"

When Kylie saw me walk in, she waved and asked if I wanted my usual.

"Yeah, banana bread and an Americano to go. And whatever this dude wants." I nodded toward Rory then went back outside to sit at one of the four bistro tables.

Rory joined me a few minutes later with our coffees and pastries. He sat down and immediately bit the top off his blueberry muffin. "So, is that barista single?"

"Kylie?" I chuckled. "No, and her boyfriend is twice your size, so I'd keep my distance."

"Noted."

I leaned back and stared straight ahead, noticing the signage from the daycare center across the street was gone and the windows had been covered up from the inside. "You know anything about that place?"

"What place?" Rory leaned forward, resting his elbows on his knees as he squinted up. "No, but it looks empty. Lemme check." He pulled out his phone and started digging around in some public records app.

I tried to recall the last time I saw activity over there, and it seemed like it had been at least a few months. "See what it's zoned for. I think the upstairs is residential like this place."

"Yeah, it is." He flipped through screens on his app and then huffed. "We missed it, but it would have been perfect. Zoned for commercial or residential...so yeah, same as here."

"Wonder who bought it." I took a sip of my coffee and looked for clues, but without being able to see inside, there wasn't much to go on. "Look up the deed and we'll see who bought it. Maybe they're planning to flip it, and we can take it off their hands at the premium. Probably still a good deal."

Rory shoved another piece of his muffin into his mouth and nodded. "Mmm-hmm."

When my curiosity was piqued, I was like a dog with a bone, and I needed to investigate further. It wasn't the greatest building ever, but the proximity to my coffee shop, my office, and to the stadium project made it particularly appealing.

And when something appealed to me, I couldn't just walk away.

Chapter 3

Poppy

"Why is this so heavy?" I took a deep breath and pushed all my weight behind the giant bookshelf that was not at all centered. It was one of the last big pieces that needed to be moved before I could start unboxing all the toys my friends and I brought into the playroom from our homes.

Of course, we all kept some things at our homes, but the playroom was designed to store all the Little stuff we didn't need to keep at home. The things we only pulled out when we were with friends or someone playing Daddy for the day.

Kylie was the only one of the Little Lovelies who had a Daddy. Daddy Troy. But according to her, he wasn't exactly the right kind of Daddy for her. She really liked him, but I had a feeling it wasn't going to last long.

But for now, if Troy came with her, he could either play with us in the main playroom or sit in the viewing room where most of the caretakers would probably stay...when we had some.

Five days ago, I closed escrow and got the keys to the building. Since then, I'd been working nonstop to get the playroom ready. I even took vacation days from my actual job as a marketing coordinator so I could paint the walls and lay foam tiles on the floor to make the playroom perfect.

Not to mention all the shopping I had to do and getting a new refrigerator brought in and meeting with the internet company and security system installers. All in all, it was a busy week, but I wanted to have the best playroom for the Little Lovelies when we met at Poppy's Place for the first time.

Tomorrow.

"Move your bottom, girl. Books aren't going to fill these shelves on their own!" I took a step back and looked at the bookshelf with my hands on my hips. It wasn't 100% centered, but Troy could move it those last few inches. It was close enough that I could set up everything around it without going crazy because it was slightly cockeyed.

I'd just started organizing our books by colored spine on the second to the bottom shelf when the alarm on my watch went off. "Seven o'clock already?" I turned to the bundle of stuffed animals that were arranged on a beanbag in one corner and asked for their input. "How did it get so late? And why didn't you tell me it was so dark in here?" I finally noticed that the sun had set and there was a dim haze in the room.

I pushed myself up to my feet from where I'd been sitting cross-legged on the floor and stretched before I went around the room and flicked on each light. Between the overhead lights and all the lamps I'd placed, it was really bright. But that was good. I needed the space to be really bright for my decorating purposes.

When my snoozed alarm went off, I pulled up a food delivery app and ordered my usual sandwich and salad from the deli down the street. The responsible thing to do would be to take a break and walk my behind down the street to pick it up and get some fresh air, but the Little part of me didn't want to be out in the dark alone. Besides, I really had a lot of work to do, so I placed my order online and turned off my alarm so I could get back to work.

Between my collections and all the books that were donated from the nine other members of the Little Lovelies club that my friends and I started a few years ago, I filled up almost all the shelves on the big bookshelf. The very bottom shelf and the upper shelf were empty, but I was really happy with how everything looked all lined up. I was so excited, I didn't even startle when the doorbell rang. Instead, I glanced at the screen at the front of the room and saw the delivery person dropping off my dinner.

"Yay! Sandwich time." As soon as I got up to grab my food from the front stoop, my tummy growled, and I realized I hadn't eaten since breakfast. I had an alarm set for lunchtime too, but when I turned it off and started to place my food order, I got distracted and never went back to it.

Now, I was really hungry.

I went through the reception area and pulled open the front door without peeking out the window to look outside. The note I left on my order was always to just ring the bell and leave the food outside, so I didn't expect to find a man standing there with my bag and milkshake in his hand. "Oh, hi." I reached for my food. "Thank you, but you could've just left it."

He grinned. "The delivery guy did leave it. I'm your neighbor, Carter Jones."

It took a moment for my brain to catch up and realize what he meant.

"Oh! Nice to meet you." I reached for my food again, not sure what he was waiting for. "Thank you for... coming to introduce yourself?"

He chuckled and handed me my dinner. "I own the coffee shop across the street and have been curious about what you're planning to put in here. Are you opening up another preschool?"

I bit my lip and could feel my cheeks heating up at that question. I couldn't tell him the truth, but I didn't like to lie. And I really had no idea what I would say even if I wanted to make up a lie. "Sorta."

The man who I finally sneaked a good look at was very tall and very attractive, especially when he smirked. "Sort of? What does that mean?"

Well, shit. I had no idea what to say to him. "Well, it's sort of like a daycare but, um, private. I mean, we aren't accepting new clients if you have kids…"

"No kids." He shook his head. "I'm single."

"Oh, me too. I mean, um, it's basically…a private playspace." My skin was burning from both embarrassment and the way it felt to have his big brown eyes skimming over every bit of it. Even though I was wearing a hoodie and leggings and had very little exposed skin, I could almost feel his gaze caressing me. It was enough to make me dizzy. "Um, thanks again for coming by." I backed up slowly, inching the door closed as I kept my gaze locked on his.

He held up his hand to stop the door before it was fully closed. "Wait, I don't think I caught your name, beautiful."

My eyes went wide at the endearment. Was he one of those guys who called everybody beautiful or… "I'm Poppy, and this is…" I took a deep breath and said it out loud to a stranger for the very first time. "Poppy's Place."

Chapter 4

Carter

Poppy's Place.

I'd been rolling those two words around in my brain for the last twenty-four hours, and my curiosity was killing me. The old signage had been removed and bright pink shutters had been installed outside of all the front-facing windows, both upstairs and downstairs. Window boxes were added to the upstairs windows, so it seemed that Poppy was moving into the full building, not just the lower retail space.

But what the hell was a private playroom anyway? I didn't know much about daycare centers, but I hadn't seen any hints of parents with babies or strollers going in or out of there. And I'd been watching the window all afternoon, doing most of my work from inside the coffee shop so I had a clear view of the shop without looking like a stalker.

Even though I totally was.

There was just something about Poppy that made me want to learn more. Maybe it was the fact that she reacted when I told her I was single by saying she was too. But that wasn't totally unusual. Lots of women would probably state their status after hearing me state mine. And why did I even say that? It wasn't my normal move to go around telling women I was single as a first introduction.

Nothing gave off creeper vibes more than desperation, but that was exactly what I was.

But it wasn't about me. It was about her. Poppy. Beautiful Poppy with her pink cheeks and red hair and big eyes that looked like they'd follow me anywhere... Even when she appeared to have been lounging on the couch or maybe painting all day, she was absolutely gorgeous.

I wanted to release the clip half holding her messy bun together and run my fingers through her locks as I gently massaged her scalp. And then I'd move my hands down her soft body, massaging everything else.

Fuck, I wasn't gonna be able to sleep until I had some answers.

As I stared out the window, Poppy emerged from her front door and looked straight at my shop, not glancing left or right before stepping off the curb and into the street. My breath hitched, and I was on my feet before she realized a car was coming and she stepped back, placing her hand over her heart as she walked twenty feet to the corner crosswalk and hit the button for the light.

My brow furrowed as I thought about what I would say to her if she were my girl. Crossing the street without looking both ways was a non-negotiable rule that would earn a good spanking if it were broken.

But she wasn't my girl. Not yet, anyway.

I sucked in a deep breath to calm my nerves and relaxed as she walked straight toward my door. Since I was tucked away in the corner, I wasn't surprised when she walked right past me and went straight to the counter. What I was surprised by was that she seemed to know Kylie, my best barista.

"Ky, can you believe it's finally today?" Poppy was bouncing on her toes in the most adorable way. From my angle, I could see her profile, and she was an absolute doll. "I'm so excited for tonight, but I'm also nervous. What if the other Little Lovelies don't like it? I think I've thought of everything, but what if I haven't? What if it's terrible?"

"Poppy, breathe. It's gonna be perfect. We're all so excited for tonight and so grateful that you're doing this for us." Kylie was getting a raise for the way she reached over the counter and grabbed both of Poppy's fidgety hands to comfort her. "We know how expensive it's all been for you to do this for us, and there's nothing that could make it terrible." She bit the inside of her cheek and looked up to the ceiling with just her eyes like she was thinking. "Except, maybe, no snacks and juice. Which I've got covered. So enjoy the next thirty minutes, get changed and in the right mindset for fun, and get ready for the greatest playdate ever."

What the hell? As I watched their interaction and listened to the words, puzzle pieces were falling into place as others were being plucked right out. I'd made some assumptions about Poppy and her business that might not have been warranted. And this new information was triggering my Daddy instincts in spades.

Little Lovelies. Snacks and juice. Mindset. Playdate.

Was it possible that Kylie and Poppy were Littles?

Kylie handed a small drink to Poppy, and as Poppy rushed to the front door to leave, I cleared my throat, making sure she heard me.

Poppy's whole body stilled as she looked over at me. It wasn't my imagination that her breath hitched as she took a step in my direction. "Oh, hi, Carter. I didn't see you over there."

"Sounds like you've got something exciting to get ready for tonight." It was on the tip of my tongue to come out and ask for details, but I was still a stranger, and I hoped she had more of a sense of privacy than to just tell me everything.

Even though I really wanted her to.

She grinned widely and wrapped both hands around her cup. "Yeah, just a little party with my friends to celebrate our new...um, house."

"That's great." I glanced over to her building. "It's looking really nice. Your shutters are very playful."

"Yay! That's what I was going for. I'm glad you think so." She glanced at her watch and bounced on her toes. "I don't mean to be rude, but I need to get back there before my friends arrive, but, um, maybe I'll see you around sometime."

"I hope so." I smiled and held her gaze, hoping she could see my interest. "Have fun tonight."

"Thank you, Carter." She turned toward the door and rushed to pull it open.

"Be careful, beautiful."

Her whole body froze again, and she slowly looked at me over her shoulder. "Yes, sir. I will."

I watched her walk to the curb and then turn to look at me through the window. She might have noticed my eyebrow raise when she turned from the edge of the street and went to the crosswalk and waited for the light to change. *Good girl.*

She was definitely submissive if not fully a Little, but I was pretty sure that private playroom of hers was exactly that. A playroom for her and her Little friends. What did she call them?

The Little Lovelies.

I definitely needed to learn more.

"Carter?" Kylie leaned over the counter closest to me. "Can I interrupt you for a moment?"

"Absolutely." I pulled my attention away from the window and walked over to the counter. "What's up?"

"Is it okay if I take the pastries we don't sell tonight? My friend is having a party, and I promised to bring snacks."

"Of course." I glanced in the display case and back at her. "Is there enough? I can order cookies or cupcakes to be delivered."

She smiled and cocked her head. "Aww, that's so sweet, Carter. But we'll be fine. There will only be eight or nine of us, so whatever we have left over here will be fine. And maybe a box of coffee?"

"Yeah, take whatever you want, Kylie." I slipped my hands into my pockets and looked back over my shoulder. "This is for Poppy's Place?"

She looked surprised by that. "Yeah, you know Poppy?"

I shrugged and tried to come across as less thirsty than I was. "We met last night. She seems really sweet."

"She's awesome." Kylie looked me over, probably trying to determine what I meant by that. "And single."

I chuckled. "She mentioned that."

"She did?" Kylie relaxed right before my eyes, and if I wasn't looking for it, I might have missed her Little tendencies too. "Yay! She's the best. And she bought that whole building for our little club to meet in. I mean, she's living upstairs, so it's also her house, but she's just so amazing."

"And very pretty." I smiled, making sure Kylie knew I was attracted to her friend.

She nodded and practically swooned right before my eyes. "I'll tell her you said so."

Chapter 5

Poppy

The cork wall was a last-minute addition I put in on Friday morning, and I was so glad I did. It was a hit, and within the first hour of our playdate, there was a beautiful collage of art covering it. Everything from coloring pages, hand-drawn pictures, and flower cutouts were the final decorations my friends and I created to make the playroom really ours.

Kylie not only brought a box full of muffins, Danishes, and banana bread from Bean Box, but she also brought Daddy Troy. Even if he wasn't the right fit for her, he was a good guy, and having a caretaker to supervise the playdate made it easier for the rest of us to really get into the headspace of being Little.

Cassie, Briana, and Willa all came together in a rideshare. They could be bratty, and it was sometimes harder for them to get back out of their Little attitude at the end of a playdate, so it was better for them to not be driving. Jasmine, Hannah, and Devyn drove themselves. As soon as everyone arrived, we broke into the snacks and started our art.

Most of us were in pretty babydoll dresses. It was our signature Little Lovelies "look." But since we were in a private space that we didn't have to clean up, we also had all our costumes and Little clothes in the closet.

Briana immediately changed into a pink onesie, and Willa took off her dress and played in a purple tank top and shorts pajama set. By the end of the night, she would probably be in just her shorts because she was a bit of a nudist when she was allowed to be free. Troy was the only Daddy present, and he was used to helping get Willa back into big girl clothes after playing so she could go home.

I wouldn't ever tell Kylie this, but Troy seemed to be the perfect kind of Daddy for someone like Willa. She needed a lot more discipline and structure than Kylie did and was constantly pushing limits without anyone around to enforce them. But Kylie and Troy were discovering their needs and would figure it out on their own.

For now, I was just so happy to have my friends around me as we had a tea party with the stuffies and read books and giggled. A lot. Eventually, we moved all the pillows and beanbags into the middle of the room, turned off the lights, and watched a cartoon.

We always took turns choosing, and it was Hannah's turn. She chose *Beauty and the Beast*, one of my favorites. I loved that Belle had her prince so close, even though she didn't know it. And when she finally figured it out, he wasn't really a beast at all. He was her perfect partner. Someday, I hoped to find someone perfect too. A perfect Daddy who would appreciate me for who I was when I was Big but also loved taking care of me when I was Little.

It was almost midnight when we finally said goodbye and everybody headed home. The best part of saying goodbye was not having to clean up anything and being able to go up into my apartment while Troy made sure everyone was able to get home safely.

When I got upstairs, I thought I'd be sleepy and ready to pass out, but I was so excited by how great the first official Little Lovelies playdate in Poppy's Place had been that I was totally wired. Instead of trying to sleep, I turned on all the lights and started unpacking the rest of my boxes.

There was still a lot to do to get my apartment the way I wanted it before I went back to work again on Monday, and midnight on Friday seemed like the perfect time to get going on it.

Chapter 6

Carter

The electrician finally closed his toolbox and looked up at me. "I spliced the wires back together, so we should be fine for now, but you're gonna need to do some serious rewiring. Old buildings like this are always gonna get you out of bed in the middle of the night for some reason or another. Here's my card." He handed me a business card even though I already had his number on my phone. "If you want a quote for the full building, let me know. If not, I don't mind the emergency after-hour visits." He chuckled. "My youngest still has two more years of college, and if you wanna cover the tuition, that's fine by me."

I rolled my eyes and faked a smile. "I bet it is. I'll give you a call during the week and you can work out an estimate. There's never a good time to shut down the store, but the work has to get done."

He nodded. "Should only be a day or two if we have all the material ready, but we always do our best to minimize disruption to your business."

"I appreciate it. And I appreciate you coming out tonight."

He grabbed the rest of his tools, and I walked him to the front door.

When I got the call from the alarm company at eleven thirty about the system shutting off, I was afraid someone had cut the lines. I was glad to know that it was just a faulty wire and not an actual burglary attempt. It was almost one in the morning, and I stretched my back as I stood in the doorway to lock up after Carl. With my back arched, I couldn't help but notice all the lights on in Poppy's apartment.

She didn't have curtains up yet, so I could see her bouncing around in her living room. I couldn't help but smile as she danced with a watering can and filled some house plants along her mantel. She was adorable. Especially in the cute little nightie she was wearing.

My eyes narrowed as I realized it was basically sheer, and I could see the perfect outline of all her luscious curves even from my spot on the other side of the street.

Annoyed that she was on display for the world to see, I surveyed the area around me, making sure nobody else was out there gawking at her the way I was.

I stepped fully outside and then leaned on the glass door with my arms folded as I continued to watch her.

That girl needed someone to remind her to be safe, especially if she would be living alone. It was a quiet street with an equal mix of businesses and residential units, but the street was totally dead at this hour, so at least I didn't have to kick any asses of strangers looking at what was mine.

Or should be mine.

Would be mine.

I was about to walk away and leave her to her chores in peace when she opened the window and leaned out to water the flowers in the planter box below it.

With the glow from her apartment backlighting her, she was almost ethereal. Her hair was down and a bit wild as it flowed around her head and shoulders in a ginger halo.

An absolute angel.

And then the little devil hopped up onto the windowsill with her ass hanging half off it and reached way over to water the planter box under the other window.

She wiggled farther out and her arm windmilled when she almost lost her balance. She caught herself when the watering can slipped out of her hand. "Whoa."

"Poppy!" I immediately crossed the street, ready to catch her if she fell.

I stood below her with the dented can on the ground at my side. "Are you okay, Poppy? Can you get back inside?"

"Uh, Carter?" She seemed shocked to see me standing below her but also a little bit relieved as she exhaled loudly. "Yeah, that was close, but I'm fine."

"Get your ass off that ledge and let me up, please, before I have a heart attack down here."

"Oh." She stared down at me, looking right into my

eyes for a long moment before she nodded and scooted back inside. "Yes, sir."

I picked up the can that wasn't completely destroyed and held it up to her.

Poppy nodded and pointed to the door. "Go in that door and turn right. Then follow the stairs up."

I heard the lock buzz, so I opened it up and headed to her apartment.

Poppy was standing at the open doorway when I approached, stuffing her arms into a zip-up hoodie. I was happy to see she had the self-awareness to know she was practically naked...but disappointed that she was covering up for me. "Thank you for bringing that up. I hope it didn't hit you."

Instead of handing her the can, I ignored her comment and leveled my sternest Daddy stare on her. "Promise you won't sit on that windowsill again. It's not safe for sweet little girls to be dangling in the air like that."

She grinned, and I could see her neck flush. "You think I'm sweet?"

The fact that she was focusing on that word was even more confirmation that she identified as Little. "I do.

And beautiful. And the kind of girl I'd like to get to know better." I handed her the can and then slipped my hands into my pockets. "Maybe I can take you to dinner tomorrow night?"

Poppy's eyes were so big and expressive as she nodded. "Okay. That sounds nice."

"But first things first." I nodded into her apartment and took a step forward so she was forced to let me in. "We need to cover those windows so no one else can get a peek of you dancing around in your little nightie."

Her arm immediately flew over her chest to cover it up as if she were still on display. "Ohmigawd! Could you see through it from all the way outside?"

I raised an eyebrow and smirked. "Vividly. And if anyone else was watching and having similar thoughts, I'd have to go kick their asses right now. So, as a community service, let's keep those perfect curves hidden from anyone who shouldn't be seeing them."

She swallowed hard and then straightened her spine, obviously deciding to be bold despite her shock at my presence. "Yes, Daddy."

She was testing me, and I liked it. I stepped right up to her, leaving just inches between her face and mine. "I like the words, but cool the attitude, Little girl, or I'll have to put you over my knee until you realize how to be safe when you're home alone."

Her emerald eyes became more black than green as lust filled her, and she nodded. "Yes, sir. I'm sorry for being sassy."

My hand went to the side of her face, cupping her cheek in my first real touch. "Don't be sorry, beautiful girl. I'm the kind of Daddy who likes a little sass. Especially when it ends with a pink bottom."

She swallowed hard and kept her eyes on me. "Noted."

As much as I wanted to pull her into my arms, me being there was probably a lot for her to take in, so I stepped back to give her some space while I took a look around the room.

Boxes were spread out and piles of stuff were on every available surface. "Do you have curtains or do we need to improvise?"

"Um...I ordered blinds, but they won't be in until next week. I was just gonna leave them open for a few more days."

I scoffed. "Not if you plan to walk around nearly naked." I reached for an empty box and held it up. "Do you have a couple more of these that I can cut up?"

Poppy nodded and hurried to her bedroom to grab some more. She returned with a stack of flattened moving boxes. "I'm done with these."

"How about some masking tape?"

She tapped her finger to her lip as she thought about it. "Will that blue painting tape work?"

"Perfectly." I pulled a small pocket knife that was attached to my key out of my pocket and began cutting up the cardboard. Eyeballing the height of the window and her petite frame of five feet nothing, I estimated we only needed to cover the lower two feet of the window to keep her shielded from prying eyes while still allowing in plenty of light and fresh air.

Within a few minutes, I had the lower portion of every window covered and a stack of cardboard remnants that I would take with me to recycle. "All right, beautiful. You should be good for tonight. Is there anything else you need before I go?"

She bit her lip as if holding back something and shook her head. "No, thank you. But what about tomorrow?"

I cocked my head, happy she was still thinking about our date. "Let me put my number in your phone so you can call me if you need anything else, and I'll plan to be here at six. Is that good?"

She smiled widely and sucked in a breath and then immediately yawned. "Yes, okay." She held her phone in front of her face to unlock it and then handed it to me.

With her camera facing her, I snapped a picture of her looking at me and sent it to myself. She was sleepy and messy and absolutely gorgeous. I wanted to give her a kiss, but it was not my place yet. Instead, before I stepped out, I held up my arms. "Can I get a hug good night?"

Poppy exhaled heavily as she practically fell into my arms and held me tight. "Good night, Carter."

I kissed the top of her head and then leaned back, trailing my finger across her cheekbone. "So now we're all the way back to you calling me Carter? We're definitely going in the wrong direction." I hoped I hadn't scared her away from anything intimate.

She looked up at me with so much innocence and desire that my cock almost burst through the front of my jeans. "If you want to be more than Carter to me, you'll have to come out and ask."

Unable to resist, I brushed the softest of kisses across her lips before I stood back. "Noted. Have a good night, beautiful girl."

I stepped out of her door and then tested the knob behind me to make sure it was locked before I headed downstairs. Even though I had no right to do it, I couldn't help peeking through the viewing room into the main playroom. My heart filled with hope and joy when I saw the playroom set up. Toys and books and stuffed animals were strewn about, evidence that the party Poppy and Kylie had been talking about was truly a playdate for Littles.

When I eventually let myself out the front door and went to my car, I knew I had to convince Poppy that she was mine.

She was my Little girl, and I was her Daddy.

Chapter 7

Poppy

Wow. Just wow.

The fact that Carter had just been standing around outside my apartment when I decided to water my plants was one thing. But then him going all Daddy on me and coming up...

Again, wow.

I'd never felt so exposed and precious all at the same time. It seemed like he really was interested in me. Not just the Big he met when I was cleaning or when I was in his coffee shop, but also the Little me who was dancing around and watering and being silly while he watched.

I looked down at my sheer babydoll nightgown and felt my skin burn with heat. He saw me practically naked... and so did anybody else outside who was looking.

At least the windows were covered now. Thanks to Carter.

It was hard for me to fall asleep because I kept thinking about Carter and all the things he said to me. He was a Daddy who liked pink bottoms. And he called me a little girl a few times.

He knew exactly what he was talking about, and everything he said got me so wet with need.

Even after I touched myself and pretended it was Daddy Carter touching me, my body was buzzing with excitement, and it took forever for me to fall asleep. Which was why I didn't wake up until after eleven on Saturday morning. I wasn't usually an early riser, but eleven was pretty late for me. Especially when I still had so much to do over the weekend.

I was about to get in the shower when I realized I had a message waiting for me on my phone. And since the name on the contact said Daddy, I instantly knew who it was from. My own father was Pop, a nickname my mom thought was funny when I was a baby, but honestly drove us crazy when she was calling out for us.

How did you sleep, beautiful girl?

My tummy fluttered with excitement at his continued use of the nickname. Especially now that he'd seen me almost naked and with a messy bun, he still wanted to be so nice to me. ***Good. Thank you. Did you sleep well?***

Other than having nightmares of a naked princess falling out her window like a clumsy Rapunzel, I had a great night.

I giggled at that. He was definitely a silly Daddy. ***I'm sorry if I made you worry. I promise not to do that again by myself.***

How about not at all. If your plants need watering, you let me know.

I responded back with a blushing emoji.

I'm looking forward to seeing you tonight. Is there anything you need help with during the day?

I'm excited for tonight too. I'm gonna do some more unpacking up here and maybe

clean up downstairs a bit before I get ready for tonight. That reminded me of something else I'd been thinking about. ***What should I wear?***

You'll be beautiful in anything, but I wouldn't mind seeing you in a cute little dress.

I cocked my head at his word choice. What did he mean by little? Did he know about my Little side or was that just his way of saying I should show a lot of skin? ***I have lots of dresses. Some for fancy parties... And some for just playing with my friends.***

The latter. But I'll be wearing nice jeans and a pullover, so anything casual is fine.

OK, Daddy. I'm looking forward to seeing you later. I felt a little nervous about calling him Daddy, but he was upfront with me, and I felt like I should be upfront with him too.

Me too, baby girl. You have no idea.

After cleaning and organizing all day, I was exhausted. I didn't even get down to the playroom, so that had to wait another day.

I laid out the dress I wanted to wear, but I didn't want to put it on too early and get it wrinkly, so I stretched out on my couch and closed my eyes for just a minute. I meant to set a fifteen-minute alarm so I wouldn't nap for too long, but I forgot and didn't wake up until I heard buzzing from my security doorbell.

I stumbled over my own feet twice before I made it to the wall panel to look at the video. Carter was standing in front of the camera with his hand held behind his back. *Oops*. I hit the button to unlock the door. "Sorry, Carter, but I'm running a bit late. I need a couple more minutes, but come on up."

I unlocked the front door and left it open a crack so he knew to come in, then I ran into the bathroom for a quick shower. I'd done all the important grooming earlier, but I'd also gotten sweaty from unpacking, so I just needed a quick rinse and once-over with my favorite snickerdoodle body wash.

I didn't have time to blow-dry my hair, so when I jumped out of the shower, I quickly towel-dried it and put it up in a French braid with some strands hanging down on both sides then slipped into the dress that was short enough to be girly, but nice enough for a restaurant. It was a pretty emerald that looked nice with my eyes. Even though it was one of my favorite dresses, I rarely had an excuse to wear it.

When I finally walked out into the living room twenty minutes later, Carter was breaking down the new empty boxes I'd thrown in the corner and had them neatly stacked by the front door.

"Oh, you didn't have to do that."

He looked back and then did a double take when he saw me. "Poppy, you look gorgeous." He walked over to me and held open his arms.

"Thanks!" I immediately stepped up to his chest and wrapped my arms around his neck, just holding on for a moment as I looked up at him. "You look nice too."

His fingers circled my neck and curled around the back of my head as he looked down at me. "I've been thinking about you all day."

I swallowed hard and nodded. "Me too. I hope this is okay for our date." I took two steps back and then twirled so the skirt of my dress fanned out.

"It's perfect for the restaurant. And maybe afterward, you can show me around Poppy's Place."

I bit my lip and could feel my eyes go wide. "Okay. If you're sure."

He reached for the side of my cheek again, his thumb brushing along my jaw. "I'm very sure, sweet girl. I want to get to know all of you."

"Do you mean...as a Daddy? Like, when I'm...Little?"

His eyes sparkled as he smiled. "That would make me very happy. When you're comfortable, I'd love to meet your Little side."

My mind was spinning at the turn of events, but I had to keep focused. Dinner first. Big-girl dinner first. And then maybe some Little girl time with a Daddy. A Daddy who wanted to play with me in my playroom.

I took a deep breath and grabbed my purse. "We should go before I fully regress." I chuckled as I hit the door. "You seem to bring that out of me."

Chapter 8

Carter

Fuck, did I want to see her regress. The little glimpses I'd caught of her Little side coming out got me hard. I wouldn't be able to stand straight when she was fully in that mindset.

So playful and carefree. Dancing around her apartment and giggling with her friends. If she allowed me to share that with her, I'd never let her go.

But first, we had dinner reservations.

We walked out to the car, and I opened the door for her, gently guiding her into the passenger seat with my hand on her back and then her elbow. Poppy was fully capable of climbing in on her own, but I wanted to touch her. And since she seemed to lean in to my touch, I took that as a good sign that she was comfortable with me.

I pulled the seatbelt strap forward and held it out in front of her. "Would you like some help with this?"

She sucked her lower lip between her teeth and nodded. "Yes, please.

I wanted to lick that lip and taste where she had bitten, but I settled for brushing the side of her cheek with my nose and whispering in her ear, "You smell delicious, sweet girl. Like cookies."

A shiver ran through her, and she shook out her shoulders as she breathed against me. "Good nose, Daddy." She caught herself and then cringed. "Sorry, that just keeps slipping out."

"Please, don't apologize. I love hearing it slip off your tongue so easily." I pulled back just enough to give her some space and looked into her eyes. "I have a feeling I could get used to hearing that for the rest of my life." I winked to lighten the moment, even though I was completely serious.

Her lip curled up in a soft grin. "That sounds nice to me too." And then her tummy rumbled, and her eyes went wide as her hand flattened over her soft belly. "Whoops. Um, excuse me. I haven't really eaten today, so I guess I'm starting to get hungry."

I frowned as I backed away and closed the door. As soon as I was in my seat, I started the engine and glanced at Poppy. "Why haven't you eaten?"

She shrugged and let out a dramatic sigh. "Too busy. Had lots of unpacking to do and... Well, I was excited for tonight."

I reached over and rested my hand on her thigh. "Excitement is not an excuse for skipping meals, beautiful. If you don't eat, you could get lightheaded or worse." My hand involuntarily gave her a squeeze. "Promise that you'll work hard to eat something healthy for breakfast and lunch, even when you're busy?"

She chuckled softly. "Why does every Daddy worry so much about mealtimes? Clearly, I'm not starving." She poked at her thigh. "I get plenty of calories just...usually all of them are between six and midnight."

I gripped her hand, and as soon as I was stopped at a traffic light, I turned and caught her eye. "Just because the outside of your body is perfect and healthy doesn't mean the inside is perfectly healthy. If you're my girl, I'll expect you to adhere to rules about healthy eating."

She scowled, and her lower lip popped out. "How healthy are we talking, because I eat a vegetable with dinner every night, but giving up french fries or muffins would be a hard limit for me."

The teasing glimmer in her eyes made me smile and shake my head. "I'd never ask you to give up things that you love, but balancing out the times that you eat and making a tiny bit of effort to throw in something green at lunch would make me very happy."

She sucked in a deep breath through her nose and blew it out slowly. "Okay, that sounds fair and...I would like to make you happy."

With that simple statement, I knew I was a goner. Poppy had me at her first slip of Daddy, and if she wanted to give up vegetables for the rest of her life, I'd have no choice but to let her. I just couldn't say no to those big green eyes.

The restaurant I chose was high-end comfort food. Something for everyone and the best baked lobster mac & cheese around. The chef was a friend of mine, so if Poppy had any allergies or food preferences, I knew he'd be willing to accommodate her requests.

But she quickly flipped through the menu and honed in on the sides section. She then closed her menu and looked up at me with those big eyes. "Are there any rules I need to follow for dinner?"

"No, beautiful. Order whatever you'd like. We'll discuss rules if you agree to be my Little girl."

She sucked in a breath and nodded as she glanced back through the menu. "Then I'd like a side of the lobster mac and cheese and the braised beef pops." She looked up at me and seemed to be debating something internally before she spoke. "Would you share the Brussels sprouts if I ordered those too?"

"I'd love to. They're delicious here."

She closed her menu and put it to the side. "Thank you."

Someone was on her best behavior. "What would you like to drink?"

She thought about it for a minute and then smiled. "A glass of bubbles, please."

"Prosecco or Champagne?"

"Prosecco. Something sweet."

When our server came, I ordered for both of us and added a bottle of Prosecco. I didn't usually drink it, but it felt like a good night to celebrate.

Chapter 9

Poppy

My dinner was yummy, and Daddy Carter even ate most of the Brussels sprouts, so I only had to have a few. That was good because I wasn't so hungry after I started thinking about showing him my playroom. He was so interested in asking me questions that I started to get even more excited. And not just happy excited but also...aroused excited.

I could feel that my panties were wet, and no amount of squirming and squeezing my thighs together satisfied the urges that were building up inside me.

"Did you save room for dessert, beautiful?"

I didn't even notice that the server had handed him a dessert menu while I was busy thinking about how much I wanted to touch myself…and him. Or have him touch me. Ugh. I needed to stop thinking that way, at least until I got back home. "I'm okay to just go back."

He cocked his head and put the menu on the side of the table with his credit card sitting on top, indicating to the server that he was ready to pay. "Is everything okay?"

I inhaled deeply and nodded at the same time. "Yes."

That darn eyebrow popped up, and his eyes narrowed. "Try again, beautiful. This time, honestly."

"I am just a little…um, excited to show you the playroom. And maybe my bedroom."

Daddy grinned and clasped his hands together on the table. "I'm excited for that too. Are you sure you're ready for that tonight?"

All sexy thoughts disappeared, and I panicked. "Oh? Is it too soon? Am I being a slut? Sorry, maybe it's too soon. Do you think I'm a slut?"

"No, sweet girl." He held out his hand and let his open palm rest right in front of me. I dropped my hand into his and took a deep breath as he gave me a squeeze. "I'd very much like to see everything you'd like to share with me, but if that's the direction you're thinking this night will go, we should probably talk about some stuff before we get to the playroom."

"Like what? I'm on the pill."

Now it was his turn to close his eyes and inhale deeply. After a moment, he looked at me with a completely straight face. "Does that mean you're sexually active with anyone else right now?"

"No!" My jaw dropped when I thought about what he was suggesting. "Of course not. I just mean, that's not something you have to worry about."

Carter nodded and his shoulders dropped a smidge. "While we're on that topic, when was the last time you were with a man?"

I scrunched up my nose, hating this part of any new relationship. "A long time ago. College, so two years ago. And it wasn't anything serious. I've mostly just had some play scenes with Daddies at the club, but those weren't sexual. And mostly they were in a group."

"Why weren't they sexual?" His tone didn't indicate any kind of judgment or anger. He just genuinely wanted to know more.

There just wasn't much more to tell. "I guess there wasn't the right kind of chemistry."

One side of his lips turned up. "And do you feel the right kind of chemistry with me?"

"Yes, Daddy," I whispered. "A lot."

His other hand slid above mine and held me in his palms, tracing my knuckles with his thumbs. "I feel it too, baby girl. And I would love to make you mine. When you're Big like right now, and I can't wait to spend time with you when you're Little too."

My breath hitched as I held back the wave of desire that pulsed through me. Was it possible to come from words alone? I didn't think so but...maybe I was about to be the first person ever. "I want that too, Daddy. Can we hurry back now?"

He nodded and slipped his card back into his wallet before leaving a stack of cash on the table. Carter stood up and reached for my hand, carefully helping me out of my seat so he could guide me out. If there weren't so many people around, I wondered if he might lift me up and carry me on his hip or over his shoulder.

A soft giggle escaped as I leaned against his side and pressed my head against his chest.

"What's so funny, baby girl?" He pushed the door open, and I stepped outside before him.

"Just thinking about how silly it'd be if you were carrying me so we can hurry back."

"Oh, you mean like this?" Before I knew it, he swept his arms beneath me and lifted me up against his chest, cradling me to him as if I weighed nothing.

I giggled again as I wrapped my arms around his neck and held on. "Put me down, Daddy. I'm too heavy."

He growled and ignored my request. "My baby girl is absolutely not too heavy for me to carry around, and I will decide when I carry you. Is that understood?"

I sighed and rested my head on his shoulder, breathing in his warm skin. "Yes, Daddy. You decide."

As soon as we were driving, my nerves started to pick up. What if he didn't like me as Little Poppy? I wasn't usually a brat, but I'd been told I could be a handful... whatever that meant.

By the time I was hitting the code to unlock the front door, a million butterflies were fluttering around in my tummy. "We didn't clean up last night, so it's kind of a mess."

I walked through the reception area to open the door to the playroom, and I did a double take. Everything had been cleaned up. Coloring books were neatly stacked, crayons were in their boxes, the stuffies were neatly arranged on the beanbags as if they were all ready to watch a cartoon together, and the dishes we dirtied from our snacktime were all cleaned and put away. "What happened?"

Daddy Carter slipped his hand up my neck and then released my braid so it fell down onto my shoulders. "What do you mean?"

"How did everything get cleaned up?" I turned to him, very confused. "When I went up, everyone was leaving, and it was a mess. The only other person who was here..." My brain finally caught up. I narrowed my eyes and put my fists on my hips. "Did you clean up?"

He shrugged one shoulder. "Maybe."

"You didn't have to do that, Daddy. We would've gotten to it. Or not. That's the good part about having this room. We don't ever have to clean up if we don't want to."

His fingers combed through my hair. Since I put it up wet, it dried in fat curls that he was separating as he massaged my scalp. "Daddy's job is to take care of his Little girl. That means cleaning up after you play with your friends."

I wanted to refute that, but...he was right. If that was the kind of Daddy he was, then it wasn't my place to question his motives. He was the one to make those decisions. "Okay. Thank you."

Carter leaned down to give me a kiss. It was soft and barely a brush of lips against lips at first, but when I moaned and wrapped my arms around his neck, hanging from him as if I needed the air from his lungs to breathe, he lifted me up and deepened the kiss. My legs wrapped around his waist, and I held on, rubbing my pussy against his abs as I tried to get as close to him as possible.

Every part of me needed to be touched, and the way his mouth moved against mine was just a tease for what it could do over the rest of my body. "Please, Daddy. I need more."

Carter kissed along my jaw and then nipped my earlobe before pulling back. "Would you like me to take care of you down here on the couch or would you like to go upstairs?"

Just the thought of him fully taking me for the first time in the playroom almost made me cry out with need. "Here. Now."

Daddy Carter chuckled and carried me to the couch. As soon as we were there, he lowered me to my feet and then spun me one hundred and eighty degrees so my back was facing him. "May I unzip your dress. It's so pretty that I don't want it to get torn or...ruined."

"Yes, Daddy. Get it off. Quick."

Daddy chuckled again and slowly unzipped the back of my dress. His hand caressed my skin on the way down, stopping just before my bottom. "Are you sure you don't want to play first? We have all night."

"No, Daddy. I need you to play with my private parts first." I could feel that my face was burning red, but I didn't care. I'd saved my virginity for the right man, and I knew with my whole heart that Carter was that man.

"Fuck, baby girl. You're making Daddy think some very naughty thoughts."

I shrugged out of the dress and turned to him, naked except for my panties. Instinctively, I covered my tummy with my arms, so he didn't see roundness there.

Daddy held his hands out wide and waited for me to mimic his movements. "Let me look at my beautiful girl."

I closed my eyes and lifted my arms out of the way, hoping he wasn't disappointed by the fact that I didn't spend much time in the gym.

"You're so beautiful, baby girl. Promise you won't ever try to hide yourself from me."

My eyes slowly opened up, and I met his gaze. The truth in his stare was obvious, so I nodded. "Okay, Daddy. I promise." I should've been more embarrassed by the fact that my breasts were exposed to him, but I could see his desire written all over his face.

He liked the way I looked, and I felt like I was floating on a cloud of cotton candy when he placed his hands on my cheeks and came in for a soft kiss. As our kisses intensified, his hand slowly moved south, teasing down my chest until he was holding each of my breasts in his large hands and running his thumbs over my nipples.

I had to squeeze my thighs together, feeling my panties get even more wet with the juice that was leaking out of me. I couldn't stop the whimper as I fisted the front of his shirt in my hands. "Please, Daddy. I need to feel you in me."

His hand lowered until it slid beneath my panties, teasing my oversensitive skin. "Right here, baby girl? Is this where you need Daddy to touch you?"

I sucked in a breath, feeling wobbly as so much sensation was zooming through my body. "Uh-huh."

"Lie back on the couch, baby. Let Daddy take care of you."

I no longer felt embarrassed about anything as I lay back on the cushions and spread my legs open for him. After standing over me for a few moments and just looking at me, Daddy kneeled on the floor and pulled my panties down my thighs until they were completely off.

At some point, I'd kicked off my shoes without even realizing it, so I was completely naked and fully on display for this man I'd barely known for a few days but had already offered my heart and body to.

Carter kissed the inside of my thigh, moving toward my center until his lips closed over the nub that had been hard and aching all night.

My back immediately bucked off the couch as I tried to get even deeper into his mouth, begging for him to give me everything. All the things I'd been saving just for him.

He continued to lick and suck and tease my clit until I was whimpering with need. "Please, Daddy. Make me feel like I'm yours."

His thick fingers entered my pussy, scraping against my channel that had only ever touched my own fingers and some small toys that felt nothing like him. His fingers slid in and out of me, and his tongue did something indescribable that took my breath away.

It didn't take more than a few minutes before I erupted, unraveling beneath Daddy's tongue as the most powerful orgasm I'd ever felt rushed through me in every direction. It was almost too much to breathe, and when I finally was able to focus again, I realized there were tears streaming down my cheeks.

"Was that okay, baby girl?" Carter kissed up my tummy, over each of my breasts, and then kissed away the tears drying on my cheeks. "Did that feel good?"

"So good." I was still floating and sleepy, but I wasn't

done. I bit my lip and looked up at him, showing him without words that I needed something else.

"What is it, baby girl? What's wrong?"

I held my hand over the one he was using to fondle my breast and gripped him tightly. "I'm still a virgin, Daddy. I need more than just your hand."

Daddy's jaw dropped as he pulled back. "You said your last relationship was sexual."

I swallowed hard, hoping he wasn't mad. "We did some sexual stuff, but not that. I've been saving that for...my Daddy."

Chapter 10

Carter

Fucking hell. A virgin. And she'd been waiting for her Daddy. *Well, sweet girl. Your wait is over.*

"Let's go up to your room, baby girl." I wrapped my hands around her full thighs and slid up to her round bottom as I lifted her into my arms. "My girl needs a proper bed to take Daddy's cock."

Poppy's arms squeezed my neck at the same time that her legs tightened around me. Her wet pussy dampened my shirt as she rocked against me. "Yes, Daddy. Take me to bed."

I groaned with need, so hard I thought I might bust right through my pants. As I carried her upstairs, her lips and hands explored every part of me that she could reach.

Poppy shoved her hand down the back of my neck, practically strangling me with my shirt so she could touch my skin, digging her nails into my muscles.

"Fuck, baby. You're making me crazy for you."

Her skin was so soft as I pressed kisses to her neck and shoulder, kneading her ass with my fingers until I carefully lowered her onto the bed. She spread out in the middle, leaning up on her elbows with her whole body on display for me.

Fuck, she was gorgeous. "Are you sure you're ready for this, baby girl? We can take things slow."

"Not slow, Daddy. I need to feel you inside me. Please." Her hands slipped down her belly and cupped the inside of her thighs, right at the apex.

As I stood watching, both of her pointer fingers moved toward her clit, touching it just enough to make her body shudder.

I pulled two condoms out of my pocket and tossed them onto the bed before stripping out of my clothes. With everything in a pile beside her bed, I crawled over her, covering her body as I hovered just high enough for her to feel my heat without bearing any of my weight. "I'm doing this now because I want to give this thing between us a real try, beautiful. I want to be your Daddy."

Poppy nodded and a sigh escaped her lips. "I think you already are."

Fuck me. I sat up just long enough to get a condom on and then smashed my mouth to hers, kissing her with so much lust and adoration I wanted to pull her right inside me so I could protect her forever.

Poppy seemed to know exactly what she needed as she spread her legs even wider and pressed her pussy up to my covered shaft. "I'm ready, Daddy. I can't wait any longer."

"This might hurt, baby girl. But I promise it'll feel good after a few minutes."

She nodded without an ounce of fear as I positioned the head of my cock at her opening and pressed in just a fraction of an inch. Poppy's mouth opened, and her breath hitched, but she kept her eyes locked on mine and nodded for me to keep going.

I kissed her again, thoroughly distracting her by massaging her plump ass while I pushed all the way inside her.

It was intoxicating to know I was touching her in a way no man ever had before and no other man ever would in the future. This girl was mine.

Once I was fully seated inside her, I held in place for a moment to give her body a chance to get used to my size. But when she started rotating her hips, circling my length with her tightness, I knew she was ready for more. "Tell me if this hurts, baby. I only want to make you feel good."

I hooked my elbows behind her knees and spread her wide as I adjusted my angle so my pelvis was hitting her clit with each thrust.

Even though she had just come on my hand, Poppy was quickly on the brink of climax after just a few moments. "Yes, Daddy. It's happening again." She grabbed both of her breasts and squeezed them, pinching her nipples and rolling them between her fingertips as I got closer to my breaking point.

"Fuck, baby girl. You're so goddamn sexy. Come when you're ready. I'm getting close too."

Poppy dug her heels into my ass, pressing me tightly to her as she rocked against me, working her clit on me as her tight pussy milked my orgasm right out of me.

My hands curled into the comforter as I tethered myself to it and to Poppy as I came inside her. My climax was intense. Longer and deeper than what I felt when I got off in the shower. It was like a bond had been created between us that I was already sure could never be broken.

Poppy came around my cock, tugging at her nipples as she screamed for Daddy. *For me.*

Neither of us were in a hurry to move after that, so I discreetly removed the condom and tossed it onto my pile of clothes on the floor, and then pulled her into my arms. Poppy naturally fit into all my corners as if she were made for me.

I stroked her hair and kissed her temple. "How are you feeling, beautiful?"

"Sleepy. And so happy."

"Would you like a bath before bed or are you ready to put on your pajamas and let me tuck you in?"

She sighed happily. "Bath sounds nice, but I don't think I can stay awake, so maybe in the morning." She opened one eye and peeked up at me. "If you're still here."

I squeezed her a little, wanting to promise that I would always be here, knowing in my heart that was true. "I'll be anywhere you want me to be, baby girl."

"Here. Right here." She closed her eyes again and shivered.

"You're cold. What would you like to wear to bed, baby girl?"

She pointed to her dresser. "Bottom drawer. You pick."

I kissed her forehead and then got up from the bed, lifting the comforter up from the side to cover her while I was gone. It wasn't really cold, but the air was cool enough that her post-orgasmic high needed warmth to stay alive a few minutes longer.

I opened her bottom drawer and my heart filled with excitement and joy at this gift she didn't even realize she was giving me. By allowing me to choose what she slept in, she was giving me permission to take care of her. There was an assortment of little nighties like the one I saw her in the night before, but I skipped over those and focused on several sets of cotton onesies. They were perfect, with just enough coverage to keep her upper body warm outside the comforter but provided easy access if my baby needed Daddy to touch her in the night.

I took the condom to the bathroom and washed up before taking a peek in her cabinets. I found the standard toiletries any young woman needed, but there was also a neat stack of diapers and an unopened pack of wipes.

On a whim, I grabbed a diaper and took it out with the wipes and sat beside my sleepy girl. "Poppy." I carded my fingers in her hair and roused her. "Let's get you dressed before I tuck you in."

She stretched her arms over her head and whined adorably. "Fine, but only because I know I'll get cold if I don't."

"How about this?" I held up a pink onesie with hearts covering it. "Is this warm enough or do you want something longer?"

"That's perfect, Daddy." She glanced down at the diaper and sucked in a breath. "Oh."

"Would you like to sleep in a diaper or panties or nothing?" I hoped she was ready to trust me with taking care of her while she was diapered, but it was a lot to ask, and I wasn't going to push her. But I knew that if she had them in her bathroom, she was comfortable with them.

"You can choose, Daddy." She looked up at me with so much vulnerability that I had to lean forward and kiss her to remind her how much I appreciated everything about her. "I don't like a diaper when I'm by myself unless I'm sad and need to be really Little. But if you're gonna stay, you can decide."

Diaper it is!

"I'm not going anywhere tonight, and I'd be honored to take care of you in every way, baby girl." I pulled back the edge of the comforter that was over her body and tugged her down by her ankles so I had better access. "Let's get you clean and warm so you can go to sleep."

She followed my hands with her eyes as I opened the wipes package and pulled out two to gently wipe her folds. I didn't come inside her, but I still wanted her to pee so she didn't risk infection. And when she did, I'd get to change her again.

The ultimate cherry on top of a perfect night with my girl.

After getting the diaper securely in place I helped her sit up so I could put the onesie over her head. "Stand up for a minute while I get you snapped."

Poppy allowed me to pull her to her feet, and I used the opportunity to admire her beauty.

"You are a vision of perfection, baby girl." I carefully pulled the ends of the onesie over her diapered bottom and got her snapped together before I pulled back the covers for her to climb between. "Is there anything else you need before I turn off the lights downstairs and make sure everything is locked up?"

She shook her head and grinned. "Just you back here."

"Give me two minutes." I rushed back down to the playroom to collect her clothes and purse and to make sure the lights were off. When I was satisfied it was safe for me to go to sleep, I went back to Poppy's room and plugged her phone into the charger by her bed before climbing in beside her.

Her arm immediately slid over my chest, and she tucked her head onto my shoulder. "What if I wet, Daddy?"

"You can wake me up to change you, or I'll take care of it in the morning. Don't worry about a thing, baby girl. Daddy's here."

Chapter 11

Poppy

As soon as I snuggled up against Daddy, I fell right to sleep, completely trusting that he would take care of anything that came up. It was maybe a bit fast to trust him that way, but Kylie had worked for him for a long time, and she trusted him with her life.

She gave me tons of examples she'd witnessed or experienced of Daddy caring for others that made me sure he was safe and would be comfortable with my Little side.

Of course, at the time she was telling me these things, she didn't know for sure if he was a Daddy or that he was looking for a Little like me. But she was confident he was into kink in some capacity based on things he'd said to her, and to me in particular, so I dropped my guard around him and let things play out naturally.

The most natural way possible, in fact, when he kissed my pussy until I had the greatest orgasm of my life and then he made love to me with such adoration that I never wanted to let him leave my side.

So when I opened my eyes on Sunday morning and saw that he was still here, I knew he was for real. I squeezed him and kissed his pec before dragging my teeth along his muscular chest.

Daddy let out a low moan and curled the arm that was around me tighter against his side. "Good morning, baby girl."

"Morning, Daddy."

His free hand immediately rubbed down my belly to the front of my diaper. When he felt the bulge, I saw the briefest hint of a smile as he turned to kiss my forehead. "Let me get you changed, unless you want a bath now?"

I couldn't hold back my excitement at getting a bath from my Daddy. "Bathtime, Daddy."

"I must have been a good Daddy last night to get such lovely rewards this morning. A wet diaper and bathtime for my baby girl." He genuinely seemed happy by what was in store for him.

Which was fine with me. This was what I'd dreamed of when I imagined having a Daddy of my very own. Carter seemed too good to be true, but whether he was or wasn't, I was gonna ride the happy Little train for as long as I could.

It was too good.

Too fun.

Too...everything. "You were a good Daddy. Very good."

He grinned and slipped out of bed, totally naked with his big dick hanging between his legs like it needed to be touched.

I didn't get a lot of time to admire it last night, but I hoped we could remedy that now. "So good that I think you deserve a bath too."

"Is that so?" Carter disappeared into the bathroom, and I heard the faucet turn on before he returned a moment later. "It might be a tight fit, but if you'd like me to join you in the tub, I think that can be arranged."

"Yes, please." I hopped up onto my knees and waited for him to reach for me and help me to my feet.

Daddy held my hand as we walked into the bathroom. Then he released the snaps on my onesie and pulled it over my head so I was standing in front of him with just the diaper. "Do you need to potty again before we take that off?"

I shook my head, slightly embarrassed but falling into my Little headspace that didn't know the meaning of embarrassment. "No, Daddy. I'm ready for my bath."

Carter nodded and expertly removed the diaper and helped me into the water. It was only about half full, but when I got in, the water got deeper. And when I scooted to the middle and Daddy slipped in behind me with two hand towels and a small bucket he must have found under my sink, the water rose to the edge without overflowing at all.

Daddy was so smart.

"No toys?" I grabbed the bucket and filled it with water then dumped it out, splashing all over my face. "Or bubbles?"

"This morning is a cleaning bath, not a playing bath, beautiful. You need to eat breakfast and drink some water or milk before it's time to play."

"Oh." I was a little disappointed, but I did need to eat. And when Daddy began to rub the soapy washcloth over my breasts and arms before washing below the waterline, I just leaned back against his chest and let all those sad feelings wash away because it felt so good to be taken care of by someone who always wanted what was best for me. "Okay, Daddy. Thank you for helping me get clean."

"Always, baby girl." He reached for the bucket that was floating in front of me and filled it with water. "Scoot forward, so Daddy can wash your hair."

I did as he asked and closed my eyes, loving the way it felt when he poured the warm water over my hair. When he added shampoo, Daddy massaged my scalp with strong fingers until there was a yummy coconut smell filling the whole room. And when it was time to wash away the shampoo, he covered my eyes with the dry towel so no suds got in them. He thought of everything. After conditioning and making sure everything was squeaky clean, it was over too soon.

"It's time to get out, baby girl. I can either make you breakfast or take you out." He leaned forward and placed a kiss on my shoulder. "What would you prefer?"

"Pancake Piazzo!" It was my favorite place for Sunday brunch. "Can we go there, Daddy?"

"Anything you want." He scooted me to the center of the tub and then stood up behind me. "Let's get you dried off and dressed so we can get some pancakes into that grumbly tummy of yours."

As if on cue, my tummy did grumble for pancakes. At least it had good taste!

Chapter 12

Carter

Every minute I spent with Poppy, I fell harder for her. I'd never had that kind of connection with a person, much less after just one night together. But I thought that meant it was real.

When you know you know, and I definitely knew. Poppy was mine.

For the next several days, I brought her lunch to make sure she didn't forget to eat it and then met up with her for dinner every night. When we went out together, she was bubbly and sweet and everything I wanted in a girlfriend. And when we were home, she easily regressed into a silly, happy, needy Little girl.

Poppy was perfect in every way.

I spent time with her in her playroom, but on Friday night, her friend group, the Little Lovelies, had another playdate planned. And she invited me to be there.

I was ecstatic, not only to get the invitation, but to get to see Poppy with her friends and in their safe space. There was just one thing I had to do first.

I was sitting in the café on Friday morning, waiting for a quiet moment to make my request. As soon as Kylie had some downtime, I went over to the counter and asked if she would mind taking a short walk with me.

"Of course, boss." She turned to Andrea and motioned toward the register. "Can you watch this? I need to go talk to Carter for a few minutes."

"You got it." Andrea was washing mugs and saucers, but there were no customers in the shop, so she would be fine if any came in.

Kylie slipped off her apron and came behind the counter. "Everything okay?"

"Yeah, I just wanted to check in with you about something that's not work related."

"Oh..." She smiled widely as if she knew exactly what

I was gonna say. "Gotcha. Can we walk down to the post office? I need to get stamps."

"Definitely." We stepped outside, and I glanced over to Poppy's. She was probably sitting at her desk with her back to the window, but I couldn't see her from my angle. "Have you had a chance to talk to Poppy recently?"

"You mean, your baby girl?" She was practically giddy as she teased me.

I chuckled and slipped my hands into my pocket. "Yes, my baby girl."

"Yeah, and I'm so happy for both of you. I don't know why I never saw it before, but you guys are perfect for each other." She turned to me, and her jaw dropped. "You're coming tonight, aren't you?"

"Yeah, that's what I wanted to talk to you about. I want to make sure you're comfortable with me being there. Obviously, I won't be there as your boss, but as your friend's Daddy, but I wanted to make sure you're alright with that."

"Yeah, of course." She waited for a woman with a stroller to pass us before she continued. "I've run into coworkers and even a few professors at kink clubs before, so I know it happens. As long as you're comfortable with it, I'm comfortable with it."

"Excellent." We approached the post office, so I opened the door for her, and she ran to the machine to buy some stamps. When she was done, I followed her back outside. "Will your boyfriend be joining tonight as well?"

"Yeah, my Daddy will be there too." She looked at me and winked. "It'll be nice for you guys to get to hang out for more than a few seconds on his way in or out of the store. And he'll appreciate having another caretaker around for when things get a little crazy. I hope you don't mind a little bit of nudity now and then. Some of us get pretty deep in our regression and forget about grown-up things like clothes and potty breaks altogether."

I laughed at that. "Yeah, Poppy warned me, and I'm ready for anything. Thank you for being so open-minded about this." I stopped and looked her in the eyes. "And thank you for telling Poppy she could trust me. I think your endorsement saved me weeks of wooing her."

"Ehh." She waved off the comment as we started walking again. "Maybe one or two dates, but definitely not weeks. You seem like you'd be a great woo-er all by yourself."

We walked the rest of the way in relative silence, with an understanding that our relationship might be about to change outside of work, but it didn't have to change anything at work.

With that final detail covered, I headed back to the office to get a few things done before heading home to shower and change for the playdate. Poppy made it clear that the Daddies could watch from afar, but she didn't expect me to play with her because her friends would be there.

That meant I could be comfortable. I put on a black t-shirt and performance joggers so I could get down on the ground to play ponies if she wanted me to, but I looked more like a bouncer than a businessman.

I got to Poppy's thirty minutes before her friends were due to arrive, and she called me from the top of the stairs as soon as I entered the stairwell.

"Daddy, I need your help!"

Taking the stairs two at a time, I rushed to her side, ready to save her from a burning building or giant rat. Instead, she shoved two scrunchies into one of my hands and a hairbrush in the other. "My braids aren't braiding right."

Her hair was parted down the center of her head with wet strands resting over each shoulder. I tried to focus on the accessories she handed to me, but I was more than a little distracted by the fact that she was wearing a diaper and nothing else. "Hey, baby girl. You look like you're almost ready to play."

She huffed and pulled both ends of her hair away from her shoulders, making her full breasts rise and heave in the most inviting way. "I'm not. My hair is all wrong."

I leaned forward and gave her a kiss then slipped my hand to her lower back and walked her to one of the dining chairs. "Sit here and let Daddy help with your braids."

She nodded and plopped dramatically into the chair. "And diapers are hard when you do it alone."

I smiled and began brushing out her hair so I could braid each side. "You could have waited for Daddy to help you…or asked me to come earlier."

"Sorry, Daddy." She reached back and squeezed my thigh. "I got excited and started without you."

Those words made me think of a different kind of excitement, but we didn't have time for that. She needed to be dressed and downstairs soon. "What else are you going to wear tonight?"

She'd mentioned her friends sometimes liked to wear just a diaper or panties but never mentioned it about herself. I was up for anything but wanted to know what to expect with another Daddy present. "My blue ducks onesie. It's new."

"Sounds adorable." I wrapped a scrunchy around her first braid then moved to the other side. "Can't wait to see it."

She nodded and then tried to turn to me before realizing it hurt when her hair was pulled. "Ouch, but I almost forgot to tell you that I'm sharing you tonight."

"You are?" I grinned, wondering what exactly that meant. "In what way?"

"Kylie always shares Daddy Troy when we need help or reminders, so I'm gonna share my Daddy in case my friends need help. Is that okay with you?"

"Of course, beautiful. I'll always help a Little girl in need." I finished the second side and stepped in front of Poppy then knelt in front of her. "What are the limits for how much help they can ask for?"

She shrugged and looked at me with the most innocent eyes. "Snack time, reading books, diaper changes. Whatever."

That was a bit more than I expected her to say, but I'd participated in plenty of caretaking scenes that weren't sexual and included bathing and diapers. "Okay, that's fine. And if there's something that makes you uncomfortable, how will you let me know?"

She cocked her head. "Like, safewords?"

I nodded, almost surprised that we hadn't had this conversation yet. We just hadn't needed to. Everything so far was natural and easy. Playing with others would be a test we both needed to be comfortable with. "What are your safewords?"

"I don't think I really need any, but I guess green, yellow, and red are fine." She crossed her arms over her chest. "Why would I need them with my friends?"

"You might not, but if I do something that you'd like me to stop, you can use your safewords. For example, if I'm giving too much attention to a friend and you need some Daddy time, you can say yellow."

She scrunched up her nose. "As long as you don't touch my friends the way you touch me when we're having sexy time, I won't be sad. But thank you for reminding me." She jumped up to her feet and wrapped her arms around my neck. "And you can use them too. If someone asks you to do something you don't want to do, just holler. Everyone is very respectful of boundaries."

"Noted, baby girl." I took her hand and walked her back to her room. "Now show me this new onesie of yours before your friends arrive."

Chapter 13

Poppy

When it was finally time to play, I was buzzing with excitement. Daddy held my hand and walked me down the stairs and then gave me a kiss in the center of the playroom. "You can start coloring, and I'll let your friends in when they arrive."

"You don't have to do that, Daddy. Every one of the Little Lovelies has a code to get in. They'll be fine on their own. You can color with me."

"All right." Daddy dropped onto his bottom beside the coffee table we used for coloring. "What would you like me to start with?"

I flipped through the stack of coloring books and found one with dancers. "Can you color a picture of me as a ballerina? I have a blue tutu that I might wear later because it'll match my ducks."

"Absolutely."

I handed him the book and a box of colors, then picked out a book for myself. I chose a teddy bear picture to draw for my Daddy. He was like a big teddy bear.

We were alone together for a few minutes, but then the other Little Lovelies started to arrive and I got distracted playing with them. Kylie and Troy also came, so Daddy got to hang out with Daddy Troy, and they seemed to keep themselves busy getting our dinner ordered and the right kind of music for a tutu dance party, which was what we all decided was most important after dinner.

By the time my friends all left, Daddy had to carry me upstairs because I was so sleepy from being so excited for so long. He cradled me in his arms, and I whispered into his ear, "I wet, Daddy."

He kissed my forehead. "I know, sweet girl. Do you want a bath or shower before bed?"

I closed my eyes and rested my head on his shoulder. "I already washed my hair, so can we just take a quick shower?"

"It would be my pleasure, baby girl."

We were at breakfast the next morning when Daddy gave me terrible news.

He had to go out of town for two nights because he had to speak at a conference far away. He asked me to go with him, but I would be stuck in the hotel room for most of the time by myself, and I had too much to do at home.

So, after spending all day with him on Saturday and having an amazing night with him, he had to catch a plane on Sunday morning.

I tried to be brave when he was saying goodbye to me, but there were still some tears. I couldn't help it. Even in just the short time we'd been together, I'd grown so attached. I liked seeing him for lunch every day and dinner every night. And waking up with him was the best.

Even if I didn't wake up with him every morning, I didn't know if I could ever fall asleep again without him tucking me in.

Devyn and Cassie came over for a playdate on Sunday afternoon, and we watched Minions and ate a lot of popcorn. Too much popcorn. By the time they went home, my tummy hurt. But Cassie also gave me some very important advice. She told me that if I didn't want my Daddy to leave, I had to give him a good reason to stay.

At first, I didn't know what that meant, but when I took a shower all by myself and had to wash all of my parts—all by myself—I got an idea.

The only real rules I had from Daddy were to eat breakfast, lunch, and dinner every day with at least two vegetables per day. And I had to make sure I didn't stay up too late by myself. Easy.

So when Daddy called at nine o'clock to tell me a story before bed, I was wearing a skimpy, babydoll nightie and no bottoms. I asked him to FaceTime me so I could see his handsome face, but it also worked well because he could see me.

I was lying in bed with the lights on and held the phone far enough away that he could see my breasts through the sheer fabric. "I miss you, Daddy." I placed my hand on my tit and gave it a squeeze before my fingers drifted lower, off the screen.

"I can see that, beautiful. What are you doing right now?"

"I was just thinking about you." I tickled my clit by brushing my fingertip over it with just enough pressure to make me feel it.

Daddy groaned and leaned back on his bed. He was wearing a button-up shirt and looked very uncomfortable. Not at all like when he was being our playroom daddy, or even better, when he was naked at home with me.

"Little girl, are you touching yourself right now?"

I bit my lip and nodded dramatically. "Yes, Daddy. I just miss you so much."

I could hear his clothes rustling in the background and wondered if he was taking out his cock too. "Good girls don't touch their pussy when their Daddy isn't around."

I shoved two fingers inside myself and rubbed the heel of my palm over my clit, pushing up to give just the right amount of pressure. A moan escaped from my throat. "Some good girls do. Wanna see?" I spread my legs wide and lowered the phone so it was pointed right at my core.

"Fuck, baby girl. You're killing me."

I pulled my fingers out and slid them through my folds, teasing my clit between them as I squeezed. Moaning again from the excitement of doing this for Daddy, I rolled my nub between my thumb and pointer finger until a spike of happy tingles shot through me. "It's killing me that you're not here. I need you to give me a special bath where your cock cleans me on the inside... And then gets me dirty all over again." I could feel my orgasm building, so I moved my hand up to my tits and squeezed my nipples, pinching the ends and pulling at them to add the sting of pain to the mix.

"Baby girl, you know Daddy owns your orgasms. You don't get to come until I tell you it's allowed." His breath was low and raspy, and I could tell by the way shoulders were shaking that he was enjoying my little show as much as I was.

My hands went back down to my opening and curled inside, searching for that special spot that Daddy knew how to find every time, but I was still looking for. "It's not as good as when you touch me here, Daddy. Tell me how to make it better. Tell me how you make me feel so good."

"Christ." He took a deep breath and then gave in to the idea. "Roll the skin around your clit over it to make it less direct stimulation, and then tap your finger over the top in a quick but steady rhythm."

I followed his instructions, and my breath hitched at how effective it was. He really did know all the tricks. I kept doing it as he watched, and when I started panting, he was panting too.

"Slip your fingers back into your pussy and get them nice and wet. Go deep and push along the inside. Feel how hot and soft and wet you are. Just slide in and out and pretend that's Daddy's big dick inside of you."

"Yes, Daddy. I love when you touch me like this." I propped the phone on my leg and used my other hand to squeeze my nipple. "You know just how to make me feel so good."

I came hard with Daddy watching from his hotel room, stroking himself until he was grunting and coming into his hand as well. It wasn't as good as when Daddy was actually with me, but it was good enough for a few days. I just hoped this traveling-without-me business wasn't gonna happen very often.

I needed my Daddy with me all the time.

Chapter 14

Carter

Being away from Poppy really sucked. I had meetings and talks scheduled from morning until night on Sunday and Monday, so at least I didn't have a lot of time to sit around and be distracted by thoughts of her. But when I did have a few moments to think about my girl, the pain in my chest was all-consuming.

I'd never been one to believe in fairytales and happily ever afters and all that nonsense, but the connection I felt to Poppy—even after sharing those first few words with her—had to count for something. Instead of worrying about what the calendar or traditions suggested was an appropriate timeline, I was moving full speed ahead with plans for my baby girl.

So far, we'd only met at her place because her playroom and all her favorite things were there. But I wanted her to be comfortable at my house too. The large Victorian I bought was meant to be an investment, but after putting a couple hundred thousand into renovations, I realized that I had basically designed it to be my dream house and just stayed in it.

It was way too big for just me, and the basement had evolved to mostly be a man cave with open space on one side if there ever were Littles who also wanted to spend time in there with us.

Poppy had her public playroom for her friends, but I also wanted her to have private space at home with me. It was important that she felt comfortable being Little in my house too, in case we wanted to start doing sleepovers there.

As soon as I dumped my luggage and took a quick shower at my place, I ordered dinner to be delivered to Poppy's and headed to grab a bouquet of flowers for her.

There was a flower shop down the street from the Bean Box, and her friend Briana worked there. When Briana saw me walk in, she eagerly clapped her hands and bounced on her toes.

"Daddy Carter. How are you?"

"I'm doing great, Briana. How are you?"

"Good. Busy until just about an hour ago." She glanced at her watch. "You have good timing."

I grinned and gestured to a small vase with a poppy bouquet in it. "Do you think Poppy would like that?"

Her eyes lit up as she nodded. "She'll love it. I always think of her wherever I'm working with poppies." Briana picked up the vase and carefully placed it on the checkout counter. "Do you want this one or something else?"

"That's perfect." I handed over my credit card. "When do you think we'll see you in Poppy's place again?"

She frowned and then blew out a sigh. "Well, things are a little up in the air for me. I might have to move." She rolled her eyes, and her lower lip popped out. "I mean, I am going to be moving. My landlord is selling the condo I'm in, so depending on where my new place is, I'm not exactly sure."

"I'm sorry to hear that, Briana. That must be stressful." I signed the receipt and lifted up the vase. "If there's anything I can do to help, just let me know. I know lots of people with rental units, so I can ask around."

She smiled and looked up at me with a sweet expression. "Thank you, Daddy Carter. Poppy is really lucky to have you."

I smiled and turned to leave. Not only did I get a cute gift for my girl, but I had a new plan brewing in my mind.

When I got to Poppy's, the delivery person with our Chinese food was there, so I grabbed the bags and punched in the door code she set up for me to let myself in. Once I got into her apartment, I expected to find her standing there waiting for me, but the front room was empty. "Baby girl, Daddy's here."

I heard a soft giggle from the bedroom, but that was it.

Apparently I was supposed to go find her.

"I guess my beautiful girl doesn't want the present I brought for her." I put the food and flowers down in her kitchen and went toward her bedroom. The door was cracked open enough to be an invitation without me being able to see inside.

"I'm in here, Daddy."

I pushed open the door and saw her wearing a bright pink tutu with ruffled panties underneath...and nothing else. Her legs were spread open with her knees wide on the comforter, a beautiful display for me to come home too.

"Hi, Daddy. I was just thinking about you."

I kicked off my shoes and took a few steps toward her as I raised an eyebrow. "Why is there a wet spot on the center of your panties, Little girl?"

She flicked one of her nipples and shrugged dramatically. "Just getting ready for you to come see me. You were gone for a very long time."

I was indeed. Instead of joining her on the bed, I sat on the edge of it and clasped my hands together over my lap. "As happy as I am to see you, my beautiful girl, I also owe you a spanking for touching yourself while I was gone... And right now."

"A spanking?" Her voice was raspy, and she tugged her panties to the side so her pink folds were fully visible to me.

Absolutely gorgeous.

I patted my lap. "Yup, let's get it out of the way so we can get to the good stuff."

She slowly got up and crawled to me before spreading herself across my lap.

The tutu was adorable, but kinda in the way. "On second thought, pull your tutu and your pretty panties down to your knees, and then get back here. I want to see your bottom turn pink as you remember why we follow our rules."

She huffed and sat up enough to push her clothes out of the way. "I'm sorry I broke the rules, Daddy. I was just thinking about you so much."

"I know, baby." I nudged her into just the right position as she lay back down so she was across my lap and with her knees slightly bent into the mattress. "I don't like to punish you either, but rules are rules."

"Rules are dumb," she whispered under her breath.

I smacked her ass, not too hard but with enough pressure to get her attention. "What was that?"

"Nothing, Daddy." She took a deep breath and pressed her forehead to the comforter. "I'll be good."

"If you need a break or to stop, you know your safewords. Otherwise, I'll give you ten swats."

She nodded and blew out the air in her lungs. "I'm ready."

I don't know that you are, baby girl.

And so I began, spanking her round cheeks, alternating the location so it wasn't ever too much pain in a single spot. Punishments were my least favorite scenes because I didn't ever want to make my subs cry. But they were important to most Littles, and Poppy had clearly been begging for this kind of attention from me.

Her shoulders shook, but she didn't ever cry out loud, so I knew she felt it but it wasn't too much.

"Nine." I ran my palm softly over her tender skin and let my fingertips dip down below her ass to her wet pussy, and I teased her opening. Then I nudged her ass in the air just a few inches and gave her one last swat right over her pussy. Not hard enough to be painful but enough to cause goosebumps to blossom across her body. "And ten. How are you feeling, baby girl?"

She sniffled and then took a stuttering breath before she wiggled her bottom. "Fine, I guess. And I'm sorry I was naughty."

My fingers slid down her crack and into her wet opening. "It seems like you enjoyed that a little too much."

She pushed back against my hand so it was deeper inside her. "It was okay."

I chuckled at her nonchalance and slid my fingers inside her a few more times before pulling out. "Well, then, let's have dinner and pack your bag. I'd like you to stay at my house tonight."

Chapter 15

Poppy

When I walked into Daddy's house, I was stunned by how big it was. He was just one person but his house was big enough for ten. "Wow, this is a nice place." I held out my arms in his foyer and spun in a circle. "I could do cartwheels in here."

Daddy laughed and reached for me when I stumbled. "Let's get some padding on the floor before you try any gymnastics in here, beautiful. I don't want you to crack your head on the marble."

I glanced down and noticed the beautiful flooring beneath my socked feet. "So pretty...but yeah, that looks like it'll hurt if I fall on it."

He looked at my feet and furrowed his brows. "Actually, socks are even more dangerous than bare tootsies, so let's take those off. If you get cold, I'll let you wear a pair of my slippers."

"I won't get cold." I lifted each foot into his awaiting palm, and he removed my socks. "I prefer to be barefoot anyway."

"Okay, then. Let me show you around, and then I'd like to talk to you about something."

He carried my overnight bag and walked me through the house. It took a while, but I mostly remembered where his bedroom was, the most commonly used bathrooms, and the kitchen. That was all I really needed.

Or so I thought until he took me down to the basement.

"Cool!" There was a bar and a huge sectional sofa in front of the biggest flat-screen TV I'd ever seen. "You have a playroom too."

"Kinda." Daddy chuckled and led me to the other side of the room. There wasn't much furniture on that side, just an empty wall and carpet. "But this is really what I wanted to show you."

I scrunched my nose as I looked around. "Do you need help decorating?"

"Yeah, I do." He pulled me into his arms, and then leaned down to kiss me. His touch was tender at first, and then he was moving with enough enthusiasm that I thought, or rather hoped, he'd lean me over the back of the sofa and fuck me right that second. But he didn't. "I'd like this to be your other playspace. For when you're here."

"Oh." I pulled back and looked at the space with a new lens. "That would be awesome, Daddy. I can put a shelf for books over here and maybe another one for my games and toys." I stepped back and held my arms out wide. "And a table for crafts and coloring can go right here. Cassie is gonna teach us how to make candles, and Kylie promised to do a cookie decorating class for the Little Lovelies." I looked up at him. "Can my friends come here too sometimes? Maybe when they have Daddies to play with you?"

He smiled and seemed to hold back a chuckle as he pushed a loose lock behind my ear. "That would make me very happy, baby girl." Daddy reached for my hand and guided me to the sofa. He sat down first and tugged me onto his lap so I was straddling him. "I love you very much, Poppy."

My heart started racing, and a boulder formed in my throat.

"I know you love your place, and I love it too, but I was wondering if you might consider living here with Daddy someday? We can wait until you're ready, or we can maybe let Briana rent your apartment if you'd like to move in sooner."

"You really love me, Daddy?" My head was spinning, and I knew he'd said lots of other stuff, but those were the words that mattered most. The only words that really mattered at all.

"I really do, baby girl. So much." He leaned forward and kissed away the tear that had somehow escaped from my left eye. "And when you're ready, I want to spend every day and every night with you."

I nodded as I sniffed back the tears that were sneaking into my sinuses. "I love you too, Daddy. I want to live with you today!"

His arms closed around me, and he rocked me on his lap for a long time before he could speak again. "I'm so fucking happy to hear that, beautiful."

I held him tightly too, replaying all the words he'd said that were finally making it through my brain. "Wait a sec. What did you say about Briana?"

"I was wondering if you even heard any of that." He laughed and nudged me back so he could look into my eyes. "I saw Briana when I bought your flowers. She said she has to find a new place to live, and since she works right down the street, I thought maybe you'd consider renting your place to her if you decide to move in with me."

I thought about it for a second and then a new wave of happiness filled me. "Yes! That's perfect. We can still have a Little Lovely protecting the playroom, and I can live here. With you. I love that idea, Daddy." I smacked a sloppy kiss onto his lips. "You're so smart!"

Epilogue

Carter

I didn't expect Poppy to agree to move in with me so quickly. Since she'd just barely moved into her new place, I figured we might be months or even a year out before she was ready to give it up.

But my girl was all in, and where we lived didn't matter as much as the fact that we were living together did. We spent the next few weeks moving out the things that she wanted to keep or leave for Briana, and then we held a huge yard sale and got rid of everything else.

Briana was so excited to move into the apartment. Not only was the mortgage Poppy was paying $100 less per month than what Briana had been paying in rent, but since she didn't have a lot of nice furniture, she was able to keep a lot of Poppy's stuff.

It made Poppy very happy to be able to help her friend save some money, keep her in the neighborhood, and have her mortgage paid in a single transaction.

My relationship with Poppy continued to grow, and within months, our dynamic had shifted from evening scenes to an almost total power exchange. She still had her job and I still had mine, of course. But after hours, she liked to hand all of her decisions and Big decisions over to me and easily let me take care of her.

She was my dream come true.

Things weren't always perfect—especially on the rare occasions when I had to travel and she wasn't able to go with me—but spending time with my Little girl and her group of Little Lovelies made my Daddy heart grow bigger than I could have ever imagined.

Cassie wants to have a Daddy of her own like Poppy and Kylie have, but she's too independent to fully submit to anyone. Even the sexy ER doctor who immediately recognizes the brat within her who needs to be tamed.

<u>Order your copy of Cassie's Candles</u> now and find out what happens to the next Little Lovely in love.

Made in United States
Troutdale, OR
09/18/2024

22923805R00070